I0600702

Birds of
a Feather

Marc Acito

A SAMUEL FRENCH ACTING EDITION

SAMUEL
FRENCH
FOUNDED 1830

SAMUELFRENCH.COM
SAMUELFRENCH-LONDON.CO.UK

FOR PRODUCTION ENQUIRIES

UNITED STATES AND CANADA

Info@SamuelFrench.com

1-866-598-8449

UNITED KINGDOM AND EUROPE

Theatre@SamuelFrench-London.co.uk

020-7255-4302

Each title is subject to availability from Samuel French, depending upon country of performance. Please be aware that *BIRDS OF A FEATHER* may not be licensed by Samuel French in your territory. Professional and amateur producers should contact the nearest Samuel French office or licensing partner to verify availability.

MUSIC USE NOTE

Licensees are solely responsible for obtaining formal written permission from copyright owners to use copyrighted music in the performance of this play and are strongly cautioned to do so. If no such permission is obtained by the licensee, then the licensee must use only original music that the licensee owns and controls. Licensees are solely responsible and liable for all music clearances and shall indemnify the copyright owners of the play(s) and their licensing agent, Samuel French, against any costs, expenses, losses and liabilities arising from the use of music by licensees. Please contact the appropriate music licensing authority in your territory for the rights to any incidental music.

IMPORTANT BILLING AND CREDIT REQUIREMENTS

If you have obtained performance rights to this title, please refer to your licensing agreement for important billing and credit requirements.

BIRDS OF A FEATHER was first produced by the Hub Theatre in Fairfax, Virginia on July 15, 2011. The performance was directed by Shirley Serotsky, with sets by Robbie Hayes, lighting by Andy Cissina, sounds by Veronika Vorel, and costumes by Deb Sivigny. The Production Stage Manager was Eric Arnold. The cast was as follows:

SILO, LOLA, BOMBSHELL, PORKEY, GAYEST, PREENING,

    ANNOUNCER, GROWN-UP TANGO . . . . .Dan Crane

ROY, PALE MALE, BOMBSHELL, BETTY, GAYER, BORED,

    TEEN TANGO, CHASTITY WRIGHT . . . . Matt Dewberry

BIRDER, GAY, FAT CAT SENATOR, MAN IN COVERALLS,

    WANNA-BE, RICHARD COHEN . . . . Eric Messner

ZOOKEEPER, PAULA ZAHN, FEMALE BIRDER . . . . Jjana Valentiner

The author wishes to acknowledge Helen Pafumi, artistic director of the Hub Theatre, who had the vision to know what this play was about before he did.

CHARACTERS

One woman and three men play 25 roles, broken down as follows:

ZOOKEEPER
PAULA ZAHN
FEMALE BIRDER

ROY
PALE MALE
BOMBSHELL
BETTY
GAYER
BORED
TEEN TANGO
CHASTITY WRIGHT

SILO
LOLA
BOMBSHELL
PORKEY
GAYEST
PREENING
ANNOUNCER
GROWN-UP TANGO

BIRDER
GAY
MAN IN COVERALLS
FAT CAT SENATOR
WANNA-BE
RICHARD COHEN

SETTING

New York City, in and around Central Park.

TIME

Early 21st Century

PLAYWRIGHT'S NOTE

This is a play about love. It's also about a bunch of other things, but if you keep love foremost in your mind, you can't go wrong. (That's true of life, as well.) So the pairings in the casting are very specific. But since love was meant to be shared, the cast of 4 actors can be enlarged up to 22.

For the emotional resonance of the play to deliver, the actors playing Roy and Silo should play Teen Tango and Grown Tango, respectively. Likewise, if you split the roles of Roy/Pale Male into two actors, you should also split the roles of Silo/Lola for balance.

If desired, the 11 principal roles can be assigned to 6 or 8 actors as follows:

> 6 actors
> > Roy / Teen Tango
> > Silo / Grown Tango
> > Pale Male
> > Lola
> > Zookeeper / Female Birder / Paula
> > Birder / Richard

> 6 actors
> > Roy / Teen Tango / Pale Male
> > Silo / Grown Tango / Lola
> > Zookeeper / Female Birder
> > Paula
> > Birder
> > Richard

> 8 actors
> > Roy / Teen Tango
> > Silo / Grown Tango
> > Pale Male
> > Lola
> > Zookeeper / Female Birder
> > Paula
> > Birder
> > Richard

As for the secondary roles, feel free to divide them up any way you wish.

You should also feel free to play around with the gender-bending casting. The point of the play is that the essential need to bond transcends not just gender, but humanity. So it makes just as much sense for a male actor to play a female bird as it does for a female actor to play a male bird. Indeed, I welcome seeing a production in which the human characters are cast gender-blind, as well.

Which leads me to a word about style. The quickest way to kill the heart and soul of my writing is to camp it up. The language is already heightened; if the performance is, too, not only do the laughs disappear, but so does the emotional connection. So don't confuse an actor playing across gender with drag, or an actor playing an animal with a cartoon.

All of the historical events of the play are true – my only flight of fancy was to wonder what these real-life animals would have felt if they had interior lives like those of humans. So the best way to figure out how the animal characters talk and move is to imagine what they would do if they were human.

These principles apply to the set and costumes, as well. I prefer you keep both as simple as possible, avoiding hyper-realism as well as caricature. My set descriptions are meant to evoke an image, not be taken literally; the same goes for projections.

Lastly, while the play is divided into two acts, it's just short enough that it can be played as one without intermission.

This play literally came to me in a fevered dream. I was in bed with the flu, unable to raise my head off the pillow, when it occurred to me that these two avian dramas (and the bird-brained human behavior they inspired) happened across Central Park from one another at the same time. As soon as I could reach for my computer, the play flowed out in that way you hear about but seldom happens. I wrote the first draft in eleven days. It was and is, as the saying goes, a labor of love.

I hope it is for you, too.

Marc

New York, June 1, 2013

For Floyd Sklaver,

My Leading Man,
First…Foremost…Forever

ACT ONE
PART ONE: MATING

SCENE ONE

(A screen full of snow. The channel changes. Images of romance appear – perhaps Ross and Rachel, Rhett and Scarlett, "You had me at hello" – click, click, click until landing on Paula Zahn on CNN. The date on the crawl reads August 25, 2007.)

ANNOUNCER. *(offstage)* And now, *Paula Zahn Now.* With Paula Zahn…Now.

PAULA. *(on screen)* We're going to spend the next hour on one of the most controversial subjects in America – gender, sexuality and what makes some people straight and others gay.

(Onstage, **PAULA ZAHN** *appears – poised, glamorous, game face on. She carries a copy of* And Tango Makes Three.*)*

PAULA. It's part of CNN's series on probing homosexuality.

(The "Probing Homosexuality" logo appears.)

A recent CNN poll on attitudes toward homosexuality shows that fully eighty-two percent of Americans are sick and tired of giving their opinions on homosexuality. But, lucky for us, there's still that eighteen percent who can't stop talking about it. So let's start by looking at the controversy over the most banned book in America for three years running, *And Tango Makes Three.*

(The cover of the book appears on the screen.)

A children's picture book about Silo and Roy, two male chinstrap penguins in the Central Park Zoo who pair-bonded and raised a chick together.

(CNN fades away as the image changes to the real penguins in the rocky landscape of the Central Park Zoo penguin house.)

PAULA. *(cont.)* This is their true story, and of the hawks who nested on the side of my building, and of the birdbrained human behavior they caused. All the facts are completely true.

Except birds can't talk.

(She and the image fade as the lights come up on a rocky landscape that slopes down to a pool of water barricaded by plexiglass and up to a wall of blue sky.)

*(**ROY** enters, an effeminate male with a big heart. To us, he appears fastidiously dressed in human clothes, but he is in fact a penguin. Using his feet, he studiously nudge-nudge-nudges a bowling ball-sized rock.)*

*(**SILO** enters, fresh from a swim. He is masculine and serious, a penguin you'd like to have a beer with. He glances nervously at the audience as he searches for someplace secluded.)*

*(**ROY** sits on the rock he's been pushing. Seeing **SILO**, he clears his throat. **SILO** doesn't pay attention. **ROY** clears his throat again.)*

SILO. You sick?

ROY. No.

SILO. It's all this recirculated air.

*(**ROY** coughs)*

See? Penguins living indoors. It's not natural.

ROY. Silo!

SILO. What?

*(**ROY** jerks his head toward the rock.)*

What?

*(**ROY** jerks his head again.)*

You've re-decorated.

ROY. Oh, c'mon.

(**ROY** *jerks his head more urgently.*)

SILO. Are we playing charades? Lemme see, one word, sounds like –

ROY. Look!

SILO. At what?

ROY. Our egg.

(**SILO** *looks at the rock.*)

SILO. That is not an egg.

ROY. Yes it is.

SILO. No it isn't.

ROY. Yes it is.

SILO. No it isn't.

ROY. That's a fine way to talk. After all, it's yours.

SILO. No it isn't.

ROY. Yes it is.

SILO. That is impossible. We are both males. And it's a rock.

ROY. *(covering the egg's "ears")* Sssh. Not in front of the c-h-i-c-k.

SILO. That is not a c-h-i-c-k. It is an r-o-c-k. You d-o-r-k.

ROY. Sticks and stones, Silo…

SILO. I am just trying to get you to face facts.

ROY. The truth isn't always black and white.

SILO. We're penguins. Everything is black and white.

ROY. *(referring upstage)* What about the Great Blue Wall?

SILO. That's not real. And neither is your egg.

ROY. I choose to believe otherwise.

(**ROY** *sits on the rock, humming "Rock-abye Baby".*)

(*From the audience, a flash bulb goes off.* **SILO** *shields himself, repelled.*)

SILO. *(to **ROY**)* What are they staring at? If they want to see a show, they should go to Times Square. *Phantom's* on twofers.

ROY. I hear *Wicked* is better.

SILO. If you like that kind of thing.

ROY. *(singing)*
   IT'S TIME TO TRY DEFYING GRAVITY...

SILO. Roy!

ROY. Jeez, who peed in your herring?

SILO. You're embarrassing me.

ROY. In front of who?

   (**SILO** *shoots him a look.*)

ROY. – m.

SILO. The featherless birds. In the dark. With the strange wings.

   (**ROY** *peers out at the audience.*)

ROY. They're called "people".

   (**ROY** *waves at the crowd.* **SILO** *knocks his hand down.*)

SILO. Sure, because all day they peep at us. Like we're freaks of nature. Just because we're both male.

ROY. They can't tell the difference. Hell, sometimes I can't tell the difference.

SILO. I can.

   (*A* **ZOOKEEPER** *enters, wearing a down vest and rubber boots, a bucket in hand. She is a Plain Jane, neither young nor old. Much in the way the penguins are at home in the water and awkward on land, she's most at home at the zoo, and off-balance in the world.*)

ROY. Please. We have no external dingle dangles. Besides, who cares if they know we're gay?

SILO. I am not gay.

ROY. Hah!

SILO. I am not. Our *relationship* is gay.

ROY. Ooh, lunchtime! Nummy, nummy, nummy.

   (*The* **ZOOKEEPER** *feeds them krill.*)

SILO. Sexual orientation is an artificial construct. A modern paradigm to codify behavior and put us in boxes.

ROY. Someone's been listening to the zookeepers.

SILO. I love you, not your gender.

ROY. Why?

SILO. That's just how I am.

ROY. No, why *me?*

SILO. Now you're fishing.

ROY. Isn't that what penguins do?

(**SILO** *wipes* **ROY***'s bib.*)

SILO. I love you because you get krill juice on your bib.

(*He refers downstage to the plexiglass.*)

I love you because you make me forget we live in a prison, trapped behind that Wall of Hard Sky.

I love you because when you look at me, you see a white bird with a black back.

ROY. Of course, silly. What do you see?

SILO. A black bird with a white front.

ROY. Huh. Never thoughta that.

SILO. That's part of your charm. Why do you love me?

ROY. Dunno. I prefer to lead the unexamined life.

SILO. So introspection is my responsibility.

ROY. And frivolity is mine. C'mon, grumpydump. This place isn't so bad. We've got each other. And room service. And soon we'll have our –

SILO. Don't say it.

(**ROY** *mouths the word* "*chick*".)

ROY. Don't you want a family?

SILO. Why? I have you.

ROY. I'm not a family.

SILO. Yes, you are. You and me makes two and us makes three. Isn't that enough?

ROY. I guess so, but I still want a –

(**SILO** *shoots a warning look.*)

– baby like creature.

SILO. Believe me, if we could have one, I would. For starters, it would be our ticket out of here.

ROY. Huh?

SILO. Haven't you noticed? Whenever any of us has a chick, the Room Service people take the whole family beyond the Great Blue Wall for a vacation. It's yet another special right rewarding heterosexual behavior.

ROY. Why do they do that?

SILO. Because if we lived in the wild as nature intended, we would move inland on our own, keeping our chicks away from the water until they were old enough to swim. But since we're stuck in this ice house, they pack us up in crates and take us on vacation until the chick is grown.

ROY. Where do we go?

SILO. We don't go anywhere.

ROY. Excuse me. Where do *they* go?

SILO. Between this prison and the next there lies the land they call the Outside.

ROY. The Outside?

SILO. Where the Great Blue Wall goes on forever and birds can fly.

ROY. Flying birds? Puhleeze.

SILO. It's true.

ROY. Then we should definitely hatch our –

SILO. Roy, you can sit on that rock as long as you want trying to turn it into an egg, but there is no magic in your ass.

ROY. I beg to differ.

(*Lights fade on* **ROY**, *leaving* **SILO** *alone with his thoughts.*)

SILO. I ask every bird who comes back from the Outside to tell me what it's like. And they talk of things called trees that extend up, up, upper still, opening onto an Everywhere of Blue where something called clouds swim on the wind. I want to see the thing they call grass and flowers and garbage. And bugs and crumbs. But most of all, I want to know everything about the bird they call Pale Male.

*(On the screen appears the image of the real **PALE MALE**, a magnificent redtailed hawk.)*

His brow so noble, his wingspan twice as wide as he is tall, his red tail soaring like a trail of blood against the Everywhere of Blue.

When I sleep, I dream of being borne on wings that double my chest in size, wings of desire that make me the envy of all the somethings below.

"Look at him up there," the somethings cry. "If only we could be him, that magnificent creature."

But that isn't the Way of the Penguin.

(He begins to peel off the trappings of his penguin clothes.)

SILO. From top to bottom, back to front, we're designed to be hidden: our bellies stark white so the predators below in the sea think we're the sunlight dancing on the water; our backs so black the predators above can't see us in the ocean depths. An entire species camouflaged. Unseen.

But underneath my slick plumage lies a cushion of air that keeps me buoyant, floating safely between the predators above and below. And in that narrow pocket I tuck away my secret self.

*(A second hawk joins **PALE MALE**, this one darker and larger. **LOLA** swoops and dives with the first, performing an aerial ballet. From offstage comes ten seconds of impassioned squawking.)*

SCENE TWO

(The image changes to reveal the cornice of 927 Fifth Avenue, an elaborately filigreed limestone building, upon which sits a huge twig nest.)

*(**PALE MALE** swoops in, a self-confident operator in an expensive clothes, a celebrity aware of his value, an Upper East Side Master of the Universe. He scans the sky, waiting for the appearance of **LOLA**, a young headturner, a trophy wife in training. She lands and they share a post-coital sigh.)*

PALE MALE. Wow, baby. You were amazing.

LOLA. No, you were amazing.

PALE MALE. No, you.

LOLA. You.

PALE MALE. You.

LOLA. You.

PALE MALE. Okay, me.

LOLA. And this nest…

PALE MALE. Those spikes are there to keep away the pigeons, but I use them to anchor the twigs.

LOLA. Genius.

PALE MALE. Just wait till we've renovated.

LOLA. We? What makes you think I'm nesting?

PALE MALE. We mated, didn't we?

LOLA. That doesn't mean we're mates. *(She looks out at the view.)* So this whole park is yours?

PALE MALE. Top of the food chain, baby.

LOLA. Must be nice.

PALE MALE. This is one of the most exclusive People Mountains on the island. You know who lives here? Paula Zahn and Mary Tyler Moore. But not together. 'Cuz they're both female.

LOLA. Wow.

(beat)

Who are they?

PALE MALE. Jeez, you are young. Paula and Mary are magical shapeshifters. They walk among us yet their phantom selves appear on the flickering light box.

LOLA. What's a flickering light box?

PALE MALE. Now you're really makin' me feel old. The featherless birds worship them in their nests. I'll show you sometime. You can see it through their Walls of Hard Sky.

LOLA. I'll check my schedule.

PALE MALE. And you know who else has been on the flickering light box?

LOLA. Me?

PALE MALE. No, me.

LOLA. You?

PALE MALE. Hell, yeah. Profiles, news reports, squawk shows…

LOLA. Are you a shapeshifter, too?

PALE MALE. Well, I don't like to brag.

LOLA. There's no need to be modest. You can't help it if you're extraordinary.

PALE MALE. You really understand me, don't you? (*He gives her a once-over.*) I can't believe how frickin' hot you are.

LOLA. I take care of myself. I fly several hours a day, eat a low-rat diet…

PALE MALE. I'm really glad you're here, Lila.

LOLA. Lola.

PALE MALE. Like I was saying, lots of hawks fly over Manhattan, but I'm the first who ever stayed and built a nest on a People Mountain.

LOLA. Get out!

PALE MALE. I'm tellin' ya, I'm a big deal.

LOLA. Is that why all the featherless birds gather across the street?

PALE MALE. Damn paparazzi. I can't go anywhere without them gaping at me: "Look! He's got a rat! Look, he caught a pigeon!" Losers.

LOLA. Do you mind the attention?

PALE MALE. It's the price of fame.

(He waves to the crowd.)

LOLA. It must be a lot of pressure – always feeling like you have to be on. Never having a private moment. It's so invasive.

PALE MALE. It can be. But I feel obligated to them.

LOLA. Why?

PALE MALE. I seem to bring some meaning to their empty lives. I mean, the things they squawk about. Have a listen at that Wall of Hard Sky.

(Lola leans against the window and the silhouettes of **RICHARD COHEN** *and* **PAULA ZAHN** *appear. Like* **PALE MALE, RICHARD** *is an Upper East Side Master of the Universe.)*

RICHARD. *(offstage)* Oh, crap, there's another hawk.

PALE MALE. That's Richard Cohen, Paula Zahn's mate. He's the leader of the people pack.

PAULA. *(offstage)* Calm down, Richard, they're not doing any harm.

RICHARD. *(offstage)* Sure, if you don't mind having Lyme disease outside your window.

PALE MALE. *(to Lola)* I don't have Lyme disease.

RICHARD. *(offstage)* Every time we walk out the front door we risk getting pelted with bloody pigeon guts and half-eaten rat carcasses.

LOLA. He says that like it's a bad thing.

PALE MALE. Those two just peck, peck, peck at each other.

RICHARD. *(offstage)* And with another one, there's bound to be chicks – again.

PALE MALE. Okay, that's enough.

RICHARD. *(offstage)* And that'll bring even more crazies staring into our windows with their telescopes.

LOLA. What did he say?

PALE MALE. You better step back.

LOLA. Why? Is Richard Cohen a predator?

PALE MALE. Don't worry. I'll protect you.

*(This impacts **LOLA**.)*

LOLA. Promise?

PALE MALE. Promise.

*(**LOLA** settles in, pleased. **PALE MALE** spreads his wings.)*

PALE MALE. So…

LOLA. So…

PALE MALE. What do you wanna do?

LOLA. What do *you* wanna do?

PALE MALE. I want to swoop around the sky with you.

LOLA. Uh-huh.

PALE MALE. Then grab your talons in mine…

LOLA. Oh.

PALE MALE. …shift your tail feathers to the side…

LOLA. Ooh, shift my feathers.

PALE MALE. Then twist my cloacal opening around yours…

LOLA. Oh, yeah.

PALE MALE. …while we hurl headlong in a death spiral…

LOLA. I love danger.

PALE MALE. Thrusting into each other…

LOLA. Yes.

PALE MALE. …for seven to ten mind-blowing seconds.

(The lights dim. In the darkness, the hawks shriek for seven to ten mind-blowing seconds.)

SCENE THREE

(The rocky landscape.)

(The ZOOKEEPER appears. When she opens her mouth to speak, it's clear she's from Staten Island, but that doesn't mean she's not smart.)

ZOOKEEPER. I went to my senior prom with Tommy Zapputi, who played the lead in our high school production of *Bye, Bye Birdie.*

That should've been my first hint.

Afterwards, we drove around in his mother's Dodge Dart, then climbed in the back seat and lost our virginity in the parking lot of the Staten Island Ferry. When we were done, he said, "Thank you. Now I know for certain that I'm gay."

So I wasn't surprised when Silo couldn't mate with a female bird.

(SILO stands awkwardly with a PENGUIN BOMBSHELL. They remain silent a long time. Finally:)

SILO. I'm sorry.

BOMBSHELL. It happens.

(The BOMBSHELL takes off her wig and hands it to SILO, who becomes the BOMBSHELL for ROY.)

ZOOKEEPER. So we tried her with Roy instead.

(ROY takes one look at her and runs screaming in the other direction.)

ZOOKEEPER. Anyone who says animals don't have feelings hasn't spent enough time with them.

It seemed really unfair to me, particularly when I had negligent birds like Betty and Porkey.

(Enter BETTY, a blowzy battle-axe in curlers and PORKEY, a bruiser in one of those beer drinking hats. BETTY tries to sit on two bowling-ball sized eggs, but she falls between them.)

PORKEY. You birdbrain.

BETTY. Who ya' callin' birdbrain?

PORKEY. You, birdbrain.

BETTY. Well, if you're so smart, you figure it out.

PORKEY. Fine.

*(***PORKEY*** *tries stacking one egg on top of the other.)*

BETTY. Careful, you'll break 'em like last time.

PORKEY. I know what I'm doing. *(He holds them in place.)* Now come sit.

BETTY. I don't think…

PORKEY. Sit, woman, sit!

(She sits on the eggs. He lets go of them, sending **BETTY** *and the eggs tumbling to the ground.)*

BETTY. Birdbrain.

(Lights dim.)

ZOOKEEPER. Luckily, my boss, Rob Gramzay – terrific guy, smart, sensitive, good-looking…gay – he saw what was happening and decided to take one of Betty and Porkey's eggs.

(The **ZOOKEEPER** *takes one egg from under a bored* **BETTY**. **PORKEY** *looks around.)*

PORKEY. Where's the other egg?

BETTY. I thought you had it.

PORKEY. Why would I have it?

BETTY. Oh, yeah, like I'm supposed to remember everything.

*(***BETTY*** *and* **PORKEY** *become* **ROY** *and* **SILO**.*)*

ZOOKEEPER. Then Rob sneaked it into Silo and Roy's nest.

(She takes **ROY***'s rock and replaces it with the egg.* **ROY** *sits down on it, humming "Rock-a-bye, Baby" while* **SILO** *glances nervously at the audience.)*

ROY. So…?

SILO. So…?

ROY. So…?

SILO. You lost weight.

ROY. No.

SILO. You changed your feathers.

> *(silence)*

> What?

ROY. Look!

SILO. Where?

ROY. It's an egg.

SILO. Not again.

ROY. No, really, look.

> *(**SILO** walks around the egg. He sniffs it. He picks it up and listens to it. Hearing something, he drops the egg in shock, but **ROY** catches it just in time, cradling it in his arms.)*

SILO. How'd you…

ROY. I don't know.

> *(They gaze in amazement at the egg.)*

SILO. It's a miracle.

> *(The lights change to a sun-dappled green, transforming the rocky landscape into the bucolic beauty of Central Park.)*

PART TWO: NESTING

SCENE FOUR

*(A **BIRDER** with a binoculars enters, an Average Joe, neither young nor old. He's from the Bronx and sounds like it, but that doesn't mean he's not smart. Most people probably underestimate him.)*

BIRDER. Two hundred and fifty days a year. That's how many times I climb into a hole in the ground, ride in an aluminum can to Manhattan that stops below a building where I go up to an office with no window. I'm like a very large mole – with computer skills. But it was one of those perfect-this-hardly-happens-in-New-York-Goldilocks kinda days - y'know, not too hot, not too cold – just right. So I decided to get a slice and take a walk in the park.

So I'm perambulatin' along the east side by the model boat pond and I see all these people set up with telescopes and binoculars, gawkin' at some building on Fifth Avenue. And at first I think, "Friggin' paparazzi, they're probably lookin' at Woody Allen's apartment" – he was havin' his technically-not-incest-but-c'mon-you-banged-your girlfriend's-daughter thing at the time – but then I see it's all kinds of people – young, old, rich, poor. Like the M-thirty bus broke down and left them all there waiting for the next one.

*(A **FEMALE BIRDER** appears.)*

BIRDER. So I ask this chick "What're ya lookin' at?" And she hands me her binoculars, which, if you think of it, was a very generous and un-New York-like thing to do, though I didn't say it at the time, which I regretted 'cuz she was nice-lookin' in a Goldilocks kinda way - not too hot, not too cold, just right. But I'm distracted because I look up and there he is.

(An image of **PALE MALE** *appears upstage. The awed* **BIRDER** *watches, well, like a hawk – suddenly still, contained, focused.)*

BIRDER. *(cont.)* A hawk – a real bird of prey – soaring back and forth in front of this swank pre-war building next to Woody's.

And, I, I, I, I couldn't breathe, I – I mean, to stand in the middle of Manhattan and see something so… well, it made me wanna, I dunno, rip off my clothes or bang a drum or get drunk and puke in the gutter or do what I did, which is just keep lookin'.

Then I look up and right above this fancy stonework with cherubs and whatnot there's this nest like eight feet wide. Do you know how much it costs to buy an apartment in that building? I do, because I have no life. Ten mill. At least. And – get this – just to be considered for the co-op you gotta have liquid assets of four times the value of the apartment. That's forty million in liquid assets. Who's got that kind of money? I can tell ya' who becuz I'm a dork. An investment banker, a hedge fund manager, television legend Mary Tyler Moore and her cardiologist husband, Doctor Robert Levine, CNN anchorperson Paula Zahn and her real estate developer husband Richard Cohen and some people who are just rich for a living. Eleven apartments on twelve floors because one of them is – wait for it – a duplex. A duplex! I live in a fifth floor walk-up in the Bronx with a bouncer named Tito who leaves pubic hair on the soap.

I tell ya', those hawks kick ass.

(He focuses his binoculars on the nest, which appears upstage.)

SCENE FIVE

*(**LOLA** sits alone. Bored. Restless. Finally, **PALE MALE** swoops in.)*

LOLA. Finally! I'm starving. Did you bring take-out?

*(**PALE MALE** drops a dead pigeon in the nest.)*

LOLA. Oh.

PALE MALE. I thought you were starving.

LOLA. I'll save it for later.

PALE MALE. You don't like pigeon?

LOLA. I asked for a squirrel. Or a rat.

PALE MALE. Pigeons are just like rats. With wings.

LOLA. *(muttering)* Tell that to your last mate.

PALE MALE. What did you say?

LOLA. Nothing.

PALE MALE. No, go ahead. You've been snapping at me all day.

LOLA. Maybe if you weren't so busy entertaining your fan club –

PALE MALE. See, just like that.

LOLA. – you'd know what the Richard Cohen is saying up here behind this Wall of Hard Sky.

PALE MALE. What's he saying?

LOLA. That I'm your fourth mate, you cloacal opening.

PALE MALE. I can explain.

LOLA. Then why did I have to hear it from him and the Paula Zahn?

PALE MALE. I've been meaning to tell you, but, what with the nest and the eggs…

LOLA. How long does it take to say "I was mated three times"? I'll tell you: less time than it took me to say it just now because, unlike me, you wouldn't have to say "How long does it take?"

PALE MALE. Calm down.

LOLA. I lose my mind for seven to ten seconds of feather-curling mid-air passion and now I'm mated to a stranger.

PALE MALE. I made your feathers curl?

LOLA. Pale!

PALE MALE. What do you want to know?

LOLA. Who were they? Where did you meet? Were you happy? How many chicks did you have? What did they like to do? Were they pretty? What happened to them?

PALE MALE. They died, okay?

LOLA. I know. I'm sorry.

PALE MALE. If you knew, then why did you ask?

LOLA. I wanted us to squawk about it.

    (**PALE MALE** *turns away.*)

LOLA. I know it must be hard...

PALE MALE. Then let's drop it.

LOLA. I would, but...

PALE MALE. But what?

LOLA. One of them ate a poisoned pigeon.

PALE MALE. Are you implying I'm a serial killer?

LOLA. You are a bird of prey.

PALE MALE. She caught it herself.

LOLA. And you're certain you can tell the difference between a healthy pigeon and a poisoned one?

PALE MALE. I'm still alive, aren't I?

LOLA. But the mothers of your chicks aren't.

    (*He picks up the pigeon and throws it off the building. The* **BIRDER** *is thrilled.*)

PALE MALE. Any other questions?

LOLA. How many children do you have?

PALE MALE. Oh...twenty.

LOLA. Whoa.

PALE MALE. Three.

(Now LOLA *turns away.)*

What?

(She starts to cry.)

That's a perfectly normal number.

LOLA. I know.

PALE MALE. Then what's wrong?

LOLA. You're like one of those Walls of Hard Sky. I can see in, but I can't touch anything. You have a whole life – three lives – that you won't share with me.

PALE MALE. Because survival is all about what's next: Find the food. Find the mate. Make the nest. Make the chicks. Find the food. Find the mate. Over and over again. Until it's over.

LOLA. Is that all?

PALE MALE. That's the Way of the Hawk. We don't fly backwards.

LOLA. Don't you ever wonder if there's anything else to life beyond eating and hunting and mating?

PALE MALE. Course not. I'm a guy.

LOLA. But I'm not.

PALE MALE. What do you want?

LOLA. I want you to look at me.

PALE MALE. I look at you.

LOLA. No you don't. Not really. You barely give me a glance as we fly in and out of the nest.

PALE MALE. My eyes are for predators and food.

LOLA. And your fans.

PALE MALE. What's that supposed to mean?

LOLA. It's lonely at the top of the food chain.

*(*PALE MALE *scoffs.)*

Don't give me that face.

PALE MALE. What face?

LOLA. This face.

(She imitates him.)

PALE MALE. You'll have plenty of company once you hatch the chicks.

LOLA. But that means even less time for our relationship.

PALE MALE. Why are females obsessed with "our relationship"?

LOLA. Oh, something about actually getting to know our life partners. We're funny that way.

PALE MALE. Fine. What do you want to squawk about?

LOLA. What you think. What you feel. What I think and feel.

PALE MALE. Okay, let's start with you.

LOLA. No, you.

PALE MALE. You.

LOLA. You.

PALE MALE. You.

LOLA. Okay, me. I think and feel… *(This is hard to admit.)* …that you don't like me very much.

PALE MALE. That's a stupid thing to say. Why would you think that?

LOLA. Because you say things like "that's a stupid thing to say."

PALE MALE. But it *is* a stupid thing to say. Of course I like you.

LOLA. Couldn't you say it nicely?

*(**PALE MALE** concentrates.)*

PALE MALE. *(nicely)* That's a stupid thing to say.

LOLA. I meant the part about liking me.

PALE MALE. Squawk is cheap, Lola. How about the thousands of things I *do* for you?

LOLA. Like what?

PALE MALE. The nest I built. The food I hunt. The eggs I babysit.

LOLA. When you're the father, it's not called babysitting. It's called parenting.

PALE MALE. I'll have you know I help out in the nest twice as much as most males.

LOLA. And the mere fact you call it "helping out" means you think it's my responsibility to sit on the eggs.

PALE MALE. It *is* your responsibility.

LOLA. Says who?

PALE MALE. Nature. Biology. Yet I'm willng to transcend that.

LOLA. Because you love sitting on your tail and getting your picture in *The New York Times*.

PALE MALE. That's not true.

LOLA. So what am I supposed to do? Applaud you for doing what's only fair? I'm not one of your fans.

PALE MALE. Those fans happen to think I'm the father of the decade.

LOLA. I'm sure you are.

PALE MALE. You don't sound convinced.

LOLA. No, I am. I just don't know what a decade is.

PALE MALE. You're just hormonal.

(She shoots him a murderous look.)

And by hormonal I mean beautiful.

LOLA. The gay penguins divide up their tasks equally.

PALE MALE. What gay penguins?

LOLA. Down in the zoo. Haven't you heard about them?

PALE MALE. Maybe. All penguins seem kinda gay to me.

LOLA. They're Central Park's newest avian celebrity dads. And they each take turns –

PALE MALE. Wait - they've got a chick?

LOLA. A little girl.

PALE MALE. Where's the mother?

LOLA. Don't know.

PALE MALE. That's not right. Two males raising a chick.

LOLA. Why not?

PALE MALE. Because a chick needs a father and a mother.

LOLA. But –

PALE MALE. I oughta know. I've done it twenty-seven times.

LOLA. I thought you said twenty-three.

PALE MALE. That chick is gonna grow up confused. Those queers could make it gay.

LOLA. I'm not sure you can make anyone gay.

PALE MALE. Exactly. You're not sure. Are you?

    (**LOLA** *ponders this, troubled*)

Are you willing to take that risk? Don't you want to do everything you can to insure our chicks grow up happy and healthy?

LOLA. Of course.

PALE MALE. Gay penguins. That's probably why so many of the featherless birds watch me from the boat pond. It's not safe for them to bring their kids to the zoo. The world's going mad down there. Black is white and up is down and no one's following the rules.

LOLA. You didn't become the first hawk in Manhattan by following the rules.

PALE MALE. That was different.

LOLA. How?

PALE MALE. It just was.

LOLA. But –

PALE MALE. Listen, sperms plus egg equals chick. Neat. Simple. Perfect. But sperms plus sperms? That just equals a sticky mess.

LOLA. Uh…ew.

PALE MALE. It's not me. It's biology. We can't change it.

LOLA. I choose to believe otherwise.

PART THREE: HATCHING

SCENE SIX

(Disco lights flash to a thumpa thumpa beat. The **ZOOKEEPER** *dances on with a cocktail. She's shed her vest and boots for some sassier clothes. She cleans up good. A* **GAY** *guy in a cowboy hat dances next to her with his arms in the air in the time-honored gay manner.)*

ZOOKEEPER. When I go to the bars with my gays and men ignore me because I don't have a penis, I can't wait for someone to finally ask me:

GAY. *(yelling)* What do you do for a living?

ZOOKEEPER. So I can say: *(yelling to him)* I'm a zookeeper.

GAY. Oh!

ZOOKEEPER. *(to audience)* Because a zookeeper is one of those jobs everyone wanted when they were five, like a fireman or a ballerina. Or a cowboy.

*(**GAY** is joined by **GAYER** and **GAYEST**. The trio bumps and grinds.)*

And, as it turns out, it's been excellent preparation for observing homosexuals in their natural habitat. Once you've studied zoology, you just can't get freaked by porn only a proctologist could love.

You see, practically every species on the planet has gay sex. But for the longest time the Straight White Men Who Rule the World tried to cover it up by calling it "dominant behavior" instead of just admitting that animals enjoy a recreational romp as much as people do. I kid you not, there are some dolphins who even take it up the blowhole.

*(**GAYEST** joins the **ZOOKEEPER**.)*

Tommy's a two-for-one deal. On the one hand, he's like my best girlfriend – someone I can talk to who understands the curative powers of a mani-pedi. On the other hand, he's like an old-fashioned boyfriend who won't sleep with me until marriage. Of course, there was the time when –

(She stops, not wanting to go there.)

ZOOKEEPER. *(cont.)* I even call him my "gay husband". Like it's the title of a sitcom. *My Gay Husband.* I can see him walking in the door at the beginning of each episode, saying:

GAYEST. Honey, I'm homo!

GAY & GAYER. *Wonh-wonh.*

*(***GAYEST*** rejoins ***GAY*** and ***GAYER.****)*

ZOOKEEPER. For Tommy, a long-term relationship means the guy stays for breakfast.

(She watches the three of them leave.)

Or guys.

(The lights and thumpa-thumpa music fade. The **ZOOKEEPER** *steps out of her heels. A* **FAT CAT SENATOR** *appears, a Strom Thurmond, Jesse Helms type.)*

ZOOKEEPER. Still, as a zoologist it makes me crazy when I hear someone say:

FAT CAT SENATOR. "Homosexuality is unnatural because it doesn't propagate the species."

ZOOKEEPER. As if our only biological reason for being on this earth was to pop out babies. Don't get me wrong, I love babies. I love the sweet smell of their heads, those pudgy little legs you just wanna mmrwahh…
When I watched Silo and Roy's chick peck, peck, peck through her shell, and part of her was in this world and part of her was in another – it was like catching a glimpse of heaven. But there are other ways to propagate a species, like genetic mutation.

FAT CAT SENATOR. Now don't start talkin' that evolution bullsh –

ZOOKEEPER. Biological diversity is nature's back-up plan.

FAT CAT SENATOR. God has a plan. When the Rapture comes –

ZOOKEEPER. We may not have enough food and water. And we'll discover that gays are necessary to survival precisely because they don't propagate the species, thus lowering the birth rate and making them available to care for post-apocalyptic orphans.

FAT CAT SENATOR. *(muttering)* Post-apocalyptic…this interview is over…

(He sludges away.)

ZOOKEEPER. It's entirely possible that having gay people – and penguins – could save lives.

*(**GAYEST** enters wearing a bathrobe and carrying a large coffee mug, which he hands to the **ZOOKEEPER**.)*

I know they saved mine.

*(They exit together as **ROY** appears with a downy gray puppet of Baby Tango, his daughter.)*

ROY. I promised myself I wouldn't be one of those annoying parents who goes on and on and on about his darling sweet snooky gookum light of his life reason for his existence, but seriously, take a look at this child. Is she not the most adorable lovable huggable creature ever ever ever ever ever in the history of the world since before the invention of time? I thought so.

(Baby Tango stirs.)

Good morning, little one. Are you hungry? Daddy will be back with food soon. It's not hard – the zoo provides room service – but it makes him feel useful, so be certain to make a big deal when he regurgitates into your throat. He's so sensitive, your daddy. You'd think I'd be the sensitive one, what with my "flighty" demeanor. But I'll let you in on a little secret. I'm actually the strong one. It's true. It comes from being very superficial. Things don't bother me much because I don't think much. It's a fool-proof system – designed by a fool. I highly recommend it.

ROY. *(cont.)* Oh, but your daddy. He's a deep thinker.
Always brooding on ideas with lots of syllables like the
inherent communistic totalitarianism of incarcerated
something something something. And he's obsessed
with our legends, like how we used to roam free at the
bottom of the world, as if it's so great to float on a
giant ice cube waiting to be swallowed by an orca. I
keep telling him, "Honey, we're here, we're queer, we
live in a zoo." And then I do my little song and dance
to cheer him up: *doo-too-doo-too-doo*. But lately, I've been
feeling so…tired. It's not your fault – well, actually it
is - but that's what it takes to be a parent. No, it's your
daddy. He looks at the walls that keep us here and
then builds more of them around himself. And I keep
tearing 'em down, day after day after day.

Then, sometimes when I'm sleeping, I'll wake up and
hear him crying in the night. And I'll open my eyes
and he's just staring at me.

*(**SILO** appears.)*

And he says:

SILO. "I love you so much…"

*(**SILO** diappears.)*

ROY. Then I'll nestle next to him, comforting him and
wondering why he loves me most when I'm sleeping.

It wasn't always like this. When we met, it was very
romantic. I was so confused. And yet not.

You see, we penguins have this ritual where we create a
mating call - a completely original song so that we can
find each other year after year in a crowd. It doesn't
matter much here in the ghetto, but it's a tradition.
And we're actually very nearsighted and can't tell each
other apart.

So we create these songs. And they – what's the word
I'm looking for? - suck. It sounds like we're gargling
kazoos.

(He demonstrates.)

Me, I prefer show tunes. I know it's sacrilegious to sing the featherless birds' songs, but I'm just a bird who can't say no.

So it was mating season and everyone was gargling away and I'm just singing to myself, the way I do…

(The lights shift to indicate a different time.)

ROY. *(cont.) (singing)*

IT'S TIME TO TRY DEFYING GRAVITY, I TH –

(He stops at the sight of **SILO**. *)*

Oh, hi.

SILO. What is that?

ROY. Show tune.

SILO. No, gravity.

ROY. I think it's a law. Preventing the featherless birds from flying.

SILO. So it's a protest song.

ROY. Do you like protest songs?

SILO. Love 'em.

ROY. It's a protest song. One of the best. A classic of the genre.

SILO. You're an odd bird.

ROY. I was hatched with a yolk on my head. That accounts for my sunny disposish.

(As they speak, **SILO** *advances on* **ROY***, who retreats, nervous.)*

SILO. You're not like the others.

ROY. I get that a lot.

SILO. I've got a secret for you.

ROY. I can't keep secrets what is it?

SILO. I'm not like the others, either.

ROY. Oh? *(He falters.)* Oh!

SILO. Something wrong?

ROY. I have a strange feeling in my cloacal opening.

SILO. Me, too.

ROY. Do you think it's contagious?

SILO. I hope so.

ROY. I need to sit down.

(**ROY** *sinks onto a rock.* **SILO** *hovers.*)

SILO. I've often thought that our black and white coats were a symbolic representation of a bifurcated nature, that the birds who adhere to the hegemonic, heteronormative model are limited in their thinking and need to expand their minds to the possibility that one could be attracted equally to both genders. What do you think?

ROY. I like your feet.

SILO. Thank you. I like...the way you sing.

ROY. Never had a lesson.

SILO. It's much better than all that penguin caterwauling.

ROY. Do you want to –

SILO. Yes.

ROY. – hear another?

SILO. There's more?

ROY. Lots.

SILO. Show me.

(**ROY** *takes a deep breath and sings:*)

ROY.

SEVENTY-SIX TROMBONES LED THE BIG PARADE...

(*The lights shift back to the present.*)

SILO. What are you doing?

ROY. Just singing to her.

SILO. Show tunes.

ROY. What can I say? We're a show-tune lovin' family.

(*He nuzzles Baby Tango.*)

(*singing*)

FISH GOTTA SWIM, BIRDS GOTTA FLY,

I'VE GOTTA LOVE ONE –

SILO. Will you shut up!

ROY. Yeesh. Someone woke up on the wrong side of the rock this morning.

SILO. Must you always make a spectacle of yourself?

ROY. It's part of my charm.

SILO. *(taking* **TANGO***)* It's not the Way of the Penguin. And it's certainly not the way for our daughter.

ROY. Why?

SILO. For starters, penguins don't fly, we swim.

ROY. Well, I can't very well sing "Birds gotta swim, fish gotta fly."

SILO. Then don't sing at all.

ROY. Okay, don't get your feathers in a bunch.

> *(beat)*

I thought you hated the Way of the Penguin: a culture of waddling conformists, a hegemoronic blahdy blah blah.

SILO. I do. (**SILO** *leans in and tickles Baby Tango.) (to Baby Tango)* And any day now, sweetheart, we'll visit the Land of Outside. Just as soon as you're up and walking, you are daddy's little ticket to adventure.

ROY. *(taking Tango back)* Ssh. Stop saying that.

SILO. Why?

ROY. It makes it sound like that's the only reason you had her.

SILO. Do you really think that? *(beat)* Is it so terrible that I'm excited to get out? That I finally have a chance to get what I want?

ROY. *(sincere)* Of course not. I'm thrilled. My dream made your dream come true. It's just that…

SILO. What?

ROY. Never mind.

SILO. Okay.

ROY. Well, if you must know, lately you've been talking a lot about this hawk: his noble brow, his wide wingspan, his red tail soaring like a trail of blood against the Everywhere of Blue. How he's so much more fascinating than this black and white colony of waddling conformists.

SILO. So?

ROY. So I'm black and white.

SILO. Sweetheart…

ROY. I know I'm being ridiculous. It's just that…you don't hold me the way you used to.

SILO. That's because you're always holding her.

ROY. *(beaming at Baby Tango)* Do you blame me?

SILO. No, she's perfect.

ROY. Do you think she looks like you or me?

SILO. Both.

ROY. Really?

SILO. She's a penguin. She looks like all of us.

ROY. *(to Baby Tango)* Don't you listen to the big, mean bird, Tango.

SILO. Tango?

ROY. That's what the keepers are calling her.

SILO. Why?

ROY. Because it takes two to tango.

SILO. Unfrigginbelievable.

ROY. What's wrong?

SILO. Don't you see? They're saying it takes two to make a chick. A male and a female.

ROY. I'm sure it's not –

SILO. Then what did they mean?

ROY. I don't know. You're the thinker.

SILO. Try.

ROY. Well, it took the two of us to hatch her. Working together. A team. And Tango Makes Three.

(singing)

WHEREVER WE GO, WHATEVER WE DO, WE'RE G –

(From the audience, a flash bulb goes off.)

SILO. I'm going for a swim.

ROY. Honey, don't be mad.

SILO. I'm not mad.

ROY. Coulda fooled me.

SILO. I'm just going for a swim, okay? That's what penguins do. We swim. At least that's what normal penguins do.

(He leaves **ROY** *and Baby Tango alone.)*

SCENE SEVEN

(The **BIRDER** *enters chomping a cigar.)*

BIRDER. I know it's kinda lame, but a bunch of us thought it'd be fun to spend Father's Day with Pale Male, y'know, 'cuz he's such a good dad.

I kinda felt obligated on account of the fact I'm sort of a regular now – it's not like I'm obsessive or anything: I only stop in on the way to work and on the way home. And sometimes during lunch. Y'know, regular. It's weird 'cuz I've never thought of myself as a regular person – I don't mean I'm special – I know I'm not – but I've always thought of myself as more of an Irregular, like the factory reject shirt with too many buttonholes.

Anyway, the other regulars are kind of irregular, too. We've got rich people from the neighborhood hanging out with street people on their way to rehab. Old people who can barely walk and young people who can barely talk. It's like nothin' else in New York. No one cares where you are in the pecking order. All that matters are the birds and how good you are at watchin' 'em.

(He looks through his binocular up on the ledge, where **LOLA** *sits. Behind her in the window, the silhouettes of* **PAULA ZAHN** *and her husband* **RICHARD COHEN** *appear.)*

LOLA. I just love to perch by the Walls of Hard Sky and watch the featherless birds inside. They have so many shiny things in their nests. I just love shiny things. And they squawk about so many topics I've never heard of: Real Estate. Alimony. Viagra. And the one they call Paula Zahn and her mate? Huuuuh, you should hear them. Just the other day he says to her:

*(***LOLA** *mouths along.)*

RICHARD. *(voiceover)* Why are you requesting an accounting of our investments?

LOLA. And she's like:

PAULA. *(voiceover)* You need to talk to my lawyer about that.

LOLA. And he's like:

RICHARD. *(voiceover)* You're just trying to break our pre-nup.

LOLA. And she's all:

PAULA. *(voiceover)* Can we please stop being so ugly and act like two people who once actually loved each other?

LOLA. And I think how lucky I am that Pale and I are so, so, so very, very happy. We have two beautiful chicks, a male and a female. We live at the best address in the city. We dine on the finest vermin. And Pale's terrific with the chicks, teaching them how to fly, leaving me time to shop for new twigs, renovate the nest…shop for more twigs. Renovate the nest. Shop…of course, sometimes I fly over the zoo to find out more about the gay penguins, but they keep them inside. Isn't that just terrible – to be a bird with no freedom.

*(The **BIRDER** lowers his binoculars.)*

BIRDER. Every week all spring, a new batch of birds shows up – two hundred and seventy five different kinds. I've lived here my whole life, I never noticed. Most New Yorkers tune out, y'know, put on that New York face…

(He demonstrates.)

…like a tank, ready to roll into a war zone. Stick on their earphones so they've got a soundtrack to the movie of their lives or blab on their cell phones to people miles away while ignoring the person next to 'em.

Ya' ever listen to other people's cell phone conversations? Most people talk about nothin'. But the Regulars, we tune in. Not just watching, but seeing. Not just listening, but hearing. We know that if a squirrel flattens himself against a tree that means one of the hawks is nearby. I once saw a mourning dove pretend to have a broken wing to distract an owl away from its nest. And I actually watched this little plover deliberately act insane just to confuse a raccoon, which is exactly what you should do when you're getting mugged.

(*The* **ZOOKEEPER** *appears.*)

ZOOKEEPER. I heard that Pale Male's chicks were getting ready to leave the nest, so I came by on my way to work. I was worried because normally birds learn to fly by hopping from branch to branch, but these little chicks are twelve stories up. There's no margin for error. But I look up and there's Pale Male swooping back and forth, buzzing around his chicks' heads, doing everything he can to encourage them to fly, showing them how and, and...

BIRDER. My dad was a bum. He walked out on us when I was four. Once in a while he'd breeze back into town just long enough to remind me how little I mattered. And to break my mom's heart one more time. He never taught me nothin' except how to hate him. So, for me, Father's Day has always been, well...not good.

But here on Fifth Avenue, there's a dad who actually cares. A dad who's teachin' his kids that to fly you've got to be willing to fall.

LOLA. And the sex! Ach, we still have it all the time. All. The. Time.

(*beat*)

Constantly. The other night, after we'd made love, we sat in the nest together, watching the flickering lights on the People Mountains, and I asked him "Why do you love me?"

(**PALE MALE** *appears.*)

PALE MALE. What kind of question is that?

LOLA. Is it so hard to answer?

PALE MALE. I never thought about it.

LOLA. Think about it now.

PALE MALE. I dunno. I guess you make me feel young.

(**PALE MALE** *disappears.*)

ZOOKEEPER. My parents still work every day crammed next to each other in one of those locksmith lean-tos in the Pathmark parking lot. They stand four feet apart but my mother SCREAMS FOR EMPHASIS to get the result she wants – typically blood spurting from the ears. When I was little, I used to think that hut was a dollhouse full of shiny things to play with – I love shiny things – but when I got older I realized that my mother is a tornado and my father the flattened trailer park you see on the news. For as long as I can remember, my pop has slept in a Barcalounger in the TV room. My ma says it's on account of his snoring, but I think he does it to get away from her.

What I don't know is whether he doesn't listen because she screams or she screams because he doesn't listen.

They would sooner die than get divorced.

BIRDER. Watchin' those chicks perched on the edge of the nest, hopping up and down, trying to work up the courage to take a flying leap into the unknown, I can't stop thinkin' of those people who were trapped in the World Trade Center. The ones who decided they'd rather leap to their deaths than burn alive. It was so horrible, but I couldn't look away. I almost felt obligated to watch, like out of respect or something. I live in the Bronx, so I saw it on TV like the rest of the world. At first I thought they were birds, their wings flapping – until I realized they were actually people tumbling and turning. For the rest of my life I'll never forget the ones who held hands as they jumped. Were they friends? Or just random people who worked in the same office? Two virtual strangers who found themselves standing above the world in a broken window, fire blazing at their backs, the wind whipping past their faces as they stared out at so much blue. And I imagine them turning to each other and saying, "Let's not die alone."

SCENE EIGHT

(Another part of the park. The **ZOOKEEPER** *enters, wheeling a cage containing* **SILO***, who watches the Outside with wonder.)*

SILO. We've stopped. Why have we stopped? I'm glad we've stopped. What can I see? Where do I look first? What's...

(And then he sees the reason: **PALE MALE** *perched above.)*

PALE MALE. Yes, it's really me.

*(***SILO*** can't speak.)*

I've been waiting for you.

SILO. Me?

PALE MALE. I said you, didn't I?

SILO. Yes. Sir.

PALE MALE. Why are you in a cage?

SILO. I'm being transported.

PALE MALE. Why don't you just fly?

SILO. My wings are vestigial.

PALE MALE. Meaning...?

SILO. They flew once. Before the invention of time.

PALE MALE. Sucks to be you. That your chick over there?

SILO. Yes.

PALE MALE. Cute.

SILO. Thank you. *(beat)* Don't eat her.

PALE MALE. I'm here to watch *my* chick.

SILO. Where?

PALE MALE. In that tree.

*(***SILO*** squints at the horizon.)*

SILO. You mean that bird getting attacked by crows?

PALE MALE. That's my little girl.

SILO. Aren't you worried about her?

PALE MALE. She's got to learn to defend herself.

SILO. Harsh.

PALE MALE. Survival of the fittest.

(**PALE MALE** *checks out* **SILO**.)

You're a gay, aren't you? Not that I have a problem with it.

SILO. That's big of you.

PALE MALE. I'm a helluva guy. *(beat)* So…?

SILO. So…?

PALE MALE. Are you?

SILO. I reject labels.

PALE MALE. That doesn't answer my question.

SILO. Actually it does. I refuse to be put in a box.

PALE MALE. But you are in a box.

SILO. Why do you want to know?

PALE MALE. I'm curious.

SILO. Really?

PALE MALE. Not like that.

SILO. I thought you didn't have a problem.

PALE MALE. I am not homophobic. I just think you're a biological malfunction that threatens the natural order of the planet. Like greenhouse gases.

SILO. I never said I was gay.

PALE MALE. You're very well-groomed.

SILO. That's the Way of the Penguin.

PALE MALE. Must be nice.

SILO. Meaning…?

PALE MALE. It's hard to be neat when you're carnivorous.

SILO. I never thought of that.

PALE MALE. The featherless birds who live beneath us complain about it all the time. You know, dropping bones and guts on their perches.

SILO. If they don't like it, they should migrate.

PALE MALE. Yeah, right. They act like they own that mountain.

SILO. How could anyone own a mountain? That's like owning the Everywhere of Blue.

PALE MALE. My feelings exactly.

SILO. *(sincere)* Yeah, right.

(That's better.)

They're a voyeuristic breed, people.

PALE MALE. You're tellin' me. They spend hours in front of their flickering light boxes, looking at their phantoms.

SILO. That's creepy. Why would they do that?

PALE MALE. I assume it's because they can't fly. *(beat)* No offense.

SILO. *(hurt)* None taken.

PALE MALE. My mates's worried they're going to take down our nest.

(Upstage at 927 Fifth Avenue A **MAN IN COVERALLS** *enters and begins to disassemble the nest.)*

But you know how females are. Actually, I guess you don't.

SILO. Actually, I do.

PALE MALE. Really? You can do that?

SILO. It's not complicated.

PALE MALE. Hang on. *(calling out)* Atta girl, Gretel. Use your claws, not your words. *(to* **SILO***)* You mind if I ask you a question?

SILO. Go ahead.

PALE MALE. Is it different with a guy? 'Cuz my mate and I argue about the dumbest stuff.

SILO. Same here. And it seems like we have the same argument over and over.

PALE MALE. Exactly. So what's the point of being a gay –

SILO. I'm not gay.

PALE MALE. Sorry. What's the point of doing a gay – if you're gonna have the same problems?

SILO. Is there supposed to be a point?

PALE MALE. Sure, or else the world doesn't make sense.

SILO. I suppose in a same-sex relationship we're not bound by the expectations of a binary gender construct.

PALE MALE. A w-w-whaty of the what?

SILO. You feel a little freer to break the rules.

PALE MALE. Just as I thought. You're a troublemaker.

SILO. Yeah. May I ask you a question?

(**PALE MALE** *nods.*)

You've had four mates -

PALE MALE. Watch it.

SILO. No offense. It's just that –

PALE MALE. Yet.

SILO. – pair bonding is such an intimate thing. How do you manage to, you know, move on from one to another?

PALE MALE. Biology.

SILO. Biology?

PALE MALE. The study of living organis –

SILO. I meant –

PALE MALE. Me, I'm full of biology. Just bursting with it. So every spring, when it's time for me have a little twist and squirt, if my mate's not around, I've got to find someone new.

SILO. Someone younger?

PALE MALE. What's that supposed to mean?

SILO. Nothing. I'm just stating a fa –

PALE MALE. I'm not like you, sweetheart. I'm stickin' with the program the way nature intended.

(*The* **MAN IN COVERALLS** *removes the last of the nest and exits.*)

You think it's okay because you live in this liberal city and the featherless birds say how cute you and your boyfriend are. But do you have any idea what they say when you're not around?

SILO. I don't get out much.

PALE MALE. That you're unnatural. You're repulsive.

SILO. Hey, there's no need –

PALE MALE. You're weak. You're nothing but a joke.

SILO. Now wait a –

PALE MALE. What's black and white and red all over?

SILO. I –

PALE MALE. A penguin who's ashamed. Why is he ashamed?

SILO. I am not –

PALE MALE. 'Cuz he's taking it in the fart box, that's why. Is that how you want people to talk about you in front of your little girl? Is it? Course not. Now watch what happens when I land on the ground.

(**PALE MALE** *alights on the ground and a flurry of flash bulbs go off.*)

Just an ordinary day for me. Being myself. Admired. Extolled. Respected. Desired. That could be you, sexy. You could be me. Would you like that? Would you like to be a celebrity instead of a curiosity?

(**SILO** *answers inaudibly.* **PALE MALE** *moves closer.*)

What did you say?

(**SILO** *whispers.*)

I can't hear you.

SILO. Yes.

PALE MALE. Yes. Then we're united. A team. You and me makes two. And us makes…

(*From offstage comes the sound of* **LOLA** *shrieking.*)

Trouble.

SILO. Don't go. Please don't –

(*But* **PALE MALE** *has gone. The* **ZOOKEEPER** *begins to pull the wagon offstage.*)

SILO. Wait, not yet. Just a little longer. I haven't… (*He darts around the cage in a panic, trying to take it all in.*) …I want…

(Upstage, the image of **PALE MALE** *swooping through the sky appears.)*

I want.

END OF ACT ONE

ACT TWO
PART FOUR: NESTING

SCENE NINE

(the rocky landscape)

ZOOKEEPER. Sure, I've been over to the model boat pond a couple of times, but I'd never seen Pale Male that close. It was like meeting the Pope or the president. He was so mesmerizing. Those intense eyes. That proud chest. His whole demeanor was so…masculine. Almost alluring.

Okay, I seriously need to get laid.

It's been so long, I'm afraid if I do I'll try to swallow the poor guy's head like a praying mantis. Or be that woman who cries after sex. Oh God, please don't let me be the woman who cries after sex. I've already passed the point of asking "What's wrong with me that I'm still single?" Now I switch between thinking I'm deficient and unlovable or that I'm sassy and self-sufficient. It's like alternate side of the street parking. Monday, Wednesday, Friday I'm a loser, Tuesday, Thursday, Saturday I'm Wonder Woman. Sunday I'm destined to be an old lady microwaving a Lean Cuisine while talking to my cockatiel Mister Wigglesworth. With occasional trips to shop for orthopedic shoes with Tommy Zaputti.

I know, it's counter-productive, but when you're single, you don't have someone else to torture, so you torture yourself.

Some women dream of having a man get on his knees and propose to her – though never while it's projected on a Jumbotron. Some fantasize about a husband who'll lounge with her in a warm tub surrounded by candles – which always looks better in the movies because they never show you getting stabbed in the back with the faucet. Me, I'm simple. I just want a nice, regular guy with a job and a brain to walk up to me and say, "Hi. I'm not gay." A guy who gets me...and my birds and my gays. And my gay birds. A straight version of Tommy, who can hold his own at a party but who'll check in periodically, touching me lightly on the neck to let me know he's back.

But then I think, "Sure, he'll like me at first because I'm not bad looking – if I've gotten enough sleep and the light is right – and I've got this job everybody wanted when they were five." But when you're in a relationship, you can't hide. It's like you're under constant surveillance.

Eventually he's gonna get up in the middle of the night and see me standing over the sink in a ratty bathrobe eating a mayonnaise sandwich.

I think of a relationship as a sea-going vessel – the Relation Ship – and I've missed the boat. It's like everyone else is on board, playing shuffleboard and eating Baked Alaska, while I'm standing alone on the dock, wondering whether my Relation Ship has hit an iceberg and sunk to the bottom of the ocean. Like the other day. We've got volunteers who handle all the school groups that come through but usually one of us keepers takes a break to answer questions. Sometimes it's a hassle because the kids can be real twits but this was a group of fifth graders from a girls' Catholic school on Staten Island. So I wanted to talk to them because these girls were me.

(Three Catholic school girls appear: **PREENING** *[the Leader],* **BORED** *[her Lieutenant] and* **WANNA-BE** *[the Wanna-Be].)*

Sorta. I gave this whole spiel about how being a zookeeper was my dream as a kid and I went to college and now I am strong, I am invincible, I am zookeeper. And I'm feeling pretty good, y'know, empowering girls to achieve their dreams, so I suddenly get all Oprah on them and ask: *(to the girls)* What's your dream? What do you want to do when you grow up?

*(**PREENING** raises her hand.)*

PREENING. I wanna be a trophy wife.

ZOOKEEPER. A trophy wife? That's your dream?

PREENING. Like yeah. You get to be rich and not work and go shopping and get hair extensions.

BORED. My mom works and she's always in a bad mood.

WANNA-BE. Or tired.

PREENING. Being a trophy wife is the best. Even if you have to have sex with some old wrinkly guy.

WANNA-BE. Like Donald Trump.

BORED. Eew! You're gonna marry Donald Trump. You're so gonna marry Donald Trump.

ZOOKEEPER. *(to audience)* And I thought, "She probably will." Because every fifteen years Trump trades in his wife for a new model. Literally. And I stood there, trying to figure out how I could possibly convey the entire feminist movement in fifty words or less when the gawky one raises her hand and says:

WANNA-BE. Are you married?

ZOOKEEPER. *(to audience)* And I looked at this poor kid, who seemed destined to spend her adolescence with her nose pressed to the glass while she watched prettier popular girls get into cars with boys, and I needed her to know that everything would be okay. That she could be happy and fulfilled with birds and gays and gay birds. So I said: *(to girls)* Yes. My husband's name is Tommy and we have two boys and a little girl: Silo, Roy and Tango makes three.

(Pop music blares as **BORED** *throws on a NY Yankees hat to become* **TEEN TANGO**, *a tomboy with that street-smart manner New York kids have.)*

TEEN TANGO. Yo, Central Park! How y'all doin'?

*(***TEEN TANGO*** waits for a response.)*

I said how y'all doin' Make some noise!

(The audience better make some noise.)

You wanna know why? You wanna know why?

(The audience better yell "why?")

'Cuz I'm Tango. And it's Tango Time!

(Tango dances. **SILO** *enters.)*

SILO. Tango!

(music stops)

(to audience) Go away. Show's over. Shoo. Shoo.

TEEN TANGO. Dad! Those are my fans.

SILO. But they're not your friends.

TEEN TANGO. Papa likes 'em.

SILO. Your papa also likes show tunes. As such, his taste is suspect.

TEEN TANGO. But we're in a book for the featherless chicks. I see them bring it all the time. We're famous.

SILO. Now you sound like papa.

TEEN TANGO. Being famous is all the featherless birds care about.

SILO. We're not featherless birds.

TEEN TANGO. You gotta see it. They catch everything I do with their magical image-capturing boxes and then right away they send my phantom all over the world-wide-world to countries and Spacebook and MyFace and the Googletube.

SILO. Why would you want that?

TEEN TANGO. Everyone wants to be known.

SILO. Not me.

TEEN TANGO. Good thing you're a penguin.

SILO. As are you.

TEEN TANGO. Don't remind me.

(**TEEN TANGO** *mimes gagging on her finger.*)

SILO. Don't you understand? We're prisoners here, held captive against our will and the laws of nature. Barricaded behind that Wall of Hard Sky for the amusement of the featherless masses.

TEEN TANGO. That's why it's the krill that we're in a book. Or on the Interblog. We've transcended the boundaries of space and time. You and I are standing here, but our phantoms are everywhere. Papa says it makes us immortal. That we're like gods.

SILO. Did I mention your papa likes show tunes?

TEEN TANGO. Daddy.

SILO. I don't care about your phantom image. I care about the real you, which is trapped right here with the real me.

TEEN TANGO. But we're not trapped. We're going on tour.

SILO. What?

TEEN TANGO. The three of us. You, me and Papa. We're in a band.

SILO. Don't be ridiculous. Animals can't play in bands.

TEEN TANGO. Ever heard of Phish?

SILO. No.

TEEN TANGO. The Monkees?

SILO. Tango…

TEEN TANGO. Snoop Dog?

SILO. What the hell's going on?

TEEN TANGO. The featherless birds say we're the most popular band in the country. They're all a twitter about it.

SILO. That can't be right.

TEEN TANGO. But I heard them: "And Tango Makes Three is the number one booked band in the country."

SILO. Booked band?

TEEN TANGO. Uh-huh.

> *(She does an air-guitar lick, then a rock star leap.)*

I love you, New York!

SILO. Listen…

TEEN TANGO. *(a heavy metal screech)* YEEEEEEEAAAAAAH!

SILO. Tango!

TEEN TANGO. Call me "Go". It's more street.

SILO. I want you to think very carefully. Are you sure they said booked band or book banned?

TEEN TANGO. Huh. Actually, neither.

SILO. That's a relief.

TEEN TANGO. They said "banned book".

SILO. I knew it!

TEEN TANGO. Don't regurgitate your lunch.

SILO. You have no idea what you're getting into. A book is a dangerous thing. And that one is making the featherless birds very angry.

TEEN TANGO. Why? Are books predators?

SILO. No.

TEEN TANGO. Do they steal your food?

SILO. No.

TEEN TANGO. Foul your nest?

SILO. No.

TEEN TANGO. Eat your young?

SILO. No!

TEEN TANGO. Then what's the problem?

SILO. Books give them ideas.

TEEN TANGO. Like what?

SILO. Like you've got two dads.

TEEN TANGO. But I do have two dads. Two gay dads.

SILO. Roy!

> *(**TEEN TANGO** stomps off.)*

ROY! Where are you?

(He looks upstage, heading toward the cornice, where he becomes **LOLA**.*)*

LOLA. Pale! Pale!

*(***PALE MALE*** *appears with some twigs, which he drops on the still empty ledge.)*

LOLA. Those won't hold.

PALE MALE. I'll make it work.

LOLA. The Richard Bird took away the pigeon spikes. Those twigs are just going to blow away.

PALE MALE. I said I'll make it work. Get some more.

LOLA. No.

PALE MALE. Get some more – please.

LOLA. Why? So you can preen for your fans?

PALE MALE. Those featherless birds are protesting our nest being taken down.

LOLA. But they're the reason the nest was taken down in the first place.

PALE MALE. Says who?

LOLA. Richard Cohen. Now there are hundreds of them down there. Even The Mary Tyler Moore Bird.

PALE MALE. Really? Where?

LOLA. There. *(shouting below)* Show's over, Mary. The hawks have left the building.

PALE MALE. Stop. Those are my fans.

LOLA. But they're not your friends.

PALE MALE. They believe in us. We represent something to them.

LOLA. They'll just have to take up a new hobby. Like harassing penguins.

PALE MALE. Now wait a sec –

LOLA. Don't lie to me. Our daughter saw the whole thing.

PALE MALE. I was trying to help him. Just because he was born a biological mutant doesn't mean he has to give in to it.

LOLA. Can you even hear how homophobic you sound?

PALE MALE. Homophobic means you're afraid of homosexuals. I'm not afraid. I'm hostile.

LOLA. And that's okay with you?

PALE MALE. Why wouldn't it be?

LOLA. You say you never fly backwards, but we're not flying forward, either. We're just going in circles.

PALE MALE. That's different.

LOLA. How?

PALE MALE. It just is.

LOLA. You're the first hawk to make a nest on the side of the People Mountain in Manhattan. If anyone can change, you can.

PALE MALE. For some fag penguins?

LOLA. For me.

PALE MALE. I'm sorry, but nature's plan is make the nest. Make the chicks. Protect the nest. Find the food.

PALE MALE/LOLA. Over and over again until –

LOLA. It's over.

PALE MALE. Exactly.

LOLA. No, I mean it, Pale. It's over.

PALE MALE. What? You don't mean -

LOLA. I can't take this anymore.

PALE MALE. Lola. Lola…

(She leaves the ledge and becomes **SILO**, *followed by* **PALE MALE**, *who becomes* **ROY**.)*

ROY. Can't take what?

SILO. This. Them. You.

ROY. Silo…

*(***ROY*** *reaches for* **SILO**, *but he shakes him off.)*

What is your problem?

SILO. My problem is that our daughter is making a spectacle of herself. My problem is that damn book. My prob –

ROY. Our daughter is proud of that book. She is proud of us. All three of us. Don't you see? I used to think that all there was to life was krill and show tunes, but now our little black and white existence means something, something bigger and brighter, something, I dunno… noble. We've become role models for alternative families all over the world-wide-world.

SILO. I don't want to be a role model. Or alternative. I don't want to be the poster child for gay rights.

ROY. Why not? You get to further the cause of justice in the world and – hello – you get to be on a poster.

SILO. It makes me uncomfortable.

ROY. Because you're gay.

SILO. No.

ROY. It wasn't a question. If it were, my voice would have gone up at the end, like "Because you're gay?" But it was a definitive statement of fact.

SILO. Except I'm not gay, our *relationship* –

ROY. – isn't gay, either. Ever since we got back from the Outside, you haven't touched me. We're like nestmates.

SILO. I'm going for a swim.

ROY. Don't you waddle away from me. I am not done with you. If you want to put up a Wall of Hard Sky between us, fine, I can take it. But our daughter is an adorable, audacious free spirit and this book has made her heart grow wings. Don't you dare try to take that away from her.

SILO. Being audacious is not the Way of the Penguin.

ROY. Screw the Way of the Penguin. Every time anyone does something remotely different you invoke the friggin' Way of the Penguin.

SILO. I don't make the rules, Roy.

ROY. But you want to break 'em as much as I do. Admit it – you want to fly "up, up, upper still" with that macho hawk you're in love with.

SILO. That's different.

ROY. How?

SILO. It just is.

ROY. No it isn't.

SILO. Yes it is.

ROY. No it isn't.

SILO. You're the one who insists on displaying our personal lives for the world-wide-world, despite the fact that I have asked repeatedly that we live a quietly subversive existence. But you can't do that. You live and breathe on that notoriety. You thrive on it.

ROY. Because the featherless birds are the only ones who pay attention to me.

SILO. Oh, so it's my fault.

(A rumbling begins, almost like a subway. But as it grows, it becomes clear that the volcanic roar is coming from upstage inside 927.)

SILO. If you were remotely honest with yourself – which I doubt – you'd admit that your need for adulation is just a way of overcompensating for the same shame you accuse me of feeling. That for all your "We're here, We're queer, We're on the cover of a book" blather, deep down in the innermost bowels of your biology you secretly fear that being gay makes you inferior. That you're unacceptable.

ROY. No.

SILO. You're an embarrassment.

ROY. No!

SILO. You're an abomination.

ROY. NO! NO! NO!

SCENE TEN

(The building begins to quake and a fissure appears down the center, cracking open like an egg to reveal the nucleus within – a tastefully appointed apartment bespeaking privilege and all the pressure that goes with it.)

(In the apartment stands Paula Zahn and her husband Richard Cohen. If they were birds, he'd be a hungry vulture and she a canary trapped in a gilded cage.)

(The roaring dies down.)

RICHARD. No way, Paula.

PAULA. You're the president of the co-op board, Richard. You've got to negotiate with these people.

RICHARD. Need I remind you that these alleged negotiators are the same crazies who've stood outside our building twenty-four hours a day? The same people who are sending us death threats?

PAULA. It doesn't matter. Those hawks have captured the world's imagination.

RICHARD. No, they've captured the world's attention.

PAULA. Exactly. Two weeks before Christmas and there's a guy down there dressed as Jesus with a sign that says, "My parents got evicted, too." The story just ran on Al Jazeera.

RICHARD. It'll blow over. Trees fall in nature and birds lose nests all the time. They're resilient animals. They'll cope.

PAULA. That's easy for you to say. You don't have CNN breathing down your neck. You don't have the tabloids calling you a hawk-hating rich bitch.

RICHARD. And of course that's the most important consideration. Never mind about what's right. Or fair.

(PAULA groans.)

What?

PAULA. Why does everything you get involved in turn into a battle?

RICHARD. Not all of us get to stay above the fray, Paula. Some of us have to roll up our sleeves and do the dirty work.

PAULA. You've just got to win, don't you?

RICHARD. You don't get a Fifth Avenue co-op by being a pussy.

PAULA. Well I'm tired of always having to apologize for you being such a dick, Richard.

RICHARD. Hey, I'm not the one having the affair.

(**PAULA** *freezes.*)

I've seen your diary.

PAULA. Oh God.

RICHARD. Paul Fribourg is one of my best friends. How could you do this?

PAULA. I know it was wrong…

RICHARD. Then why did you do it?

PAULA. I got tired. Of us. Of this.

RICHARD. How do you think I feel, being the schmuck holding the purse while some a-hole with a camera says, "Could you step aside for the picture, Mister Zahn?" I'm your husband, not your lackey.

PAULA. You knew what you were getting into when we got married.

RICHARD. So did you.

PAULA. But when's the last time you actually looked at me?

RICHARD. Millions of people look at you. You don't need another fan.

PAULA. Once in a while it'd be nice if you showed me you cared.

RICHARD. Show you I cared? Twenty years ago you came into this marriage with a net worth of exactly two hundred and fifty thousand dollars and I busted my hump turning it into twenty-five million. I made our life possible so all you had to worry about was your precious job.

PAULA. And raising your children.

RICHARD. You and the nanny.

PAULA. You do not want to talk about parenting.

RICHARD. I think I do.

PAULA. What's that supposed to mean?

RICHARD. I'm not the one who found your diary.

PAULA. What?

RICHARD. Haley did.

PAULA. Oh, God...

RICHARD. That's right. I found out you were screwing my friend – excuse me, my ex-friend – from our seventeen-year-old daughter.

PAULA. I'm going to be sick.

(**PAULA** *flees.*)

RICHARD. While you're at it, why don't you call off your lawyer? (**RICHARD** *deflates, exhausted.*) Now who's the dick?

SCENE ELEVEN

(Upstage the CNN Logo appears. **PAULA** *reenters, game face on.)*

ANNOUNCER. *(offstage)* And now, back to *Paula Zahn Now.* With Paula Zahn...Now.

PAULA. As part of our continuing series on Probing Homosexuality, let's turn to Loudoun County, Virginia.

*(***CHASTITY*** *enters, a helicopter mom with especially sharp blades. She pushes a library cart full of books.)*

Chastity Wright volunteers at her school library. She shelves books...

*(***CHASTITY*** *uses hand sanitizer.)*

PAULA. She tidies up.

(She takes a book from the cart.)

She reads at storytime.

CHASTITY. This story is called *Peter Pan Peanut Allergies...*

PAULA. But Chastity has never engaged in any controversy until she encountered this book:

(On the wall, the cover of And Tango Makes Three *appears.)*

*(***CHASTITY*** *pulls a copy of it off the cart and cleans it.)*

*(***PAULA*** *turns to her.)*

Chastity, why do you object so strongly to this book?

CHASTITY. Well, Diane...

PAULA. Paula.

CHASTITY. Aren't you you Diane Sawyer?

PAULA. I'm Paula Zahn. From CNN.

CHASTITY. Oh, so this is cable.

PAULA. Chastity, why do you object so strongly to this book?

CHASTITY. Well...

(She hesitates. **PAULA** *mouths "Paula".)*

…Paula. I'm just a mom. I'm you. You're me. We're us. And us's like us need to look out for our little thems, don't we? So I think conversations about "alternative" families belong at home. Behind closed doors. But how am I supposed to teach family values to my children when it doesn't say anywhere on this book that it's about homosexuality?

PAULA. Nowhere?

CHASTITY. Nowhere. Not on the back. Not on the jacket. You don't know until you're several pages into it that it's about two males raising a chick. It's a bait-and-switch. That's why I would just like to see the book removed from the shelves and placed in a special area for sensitive material.

Or at the very least, mark it with a small red dot to indicate that it's controversial.

(She flips the book over to reveal an enormous red circle on the back with a slash through it.)

PAULA. But isn't the job of the library to make information available, not take over the role of the parent and decide who has access to it?

CHASTITY. We don't put pornography in the school libraries.

PAULA. This is hardly pornography.

CHASTITY. It says the penguins "sleep together".

PAULA. So do Curious George and the Man in the Yellow Hat.

CHASTITY. Really? *(beat)* You're that hawk-hating rich bitch, aren't you?

PAULA. So what do you say to those gay parents who feel that their lifestyle should be represented, too?

CHASTITY. What do you mean?

PAULA. Let's say there's a lesbian couple with a child in your school.

CHASTITY. That's just silly. This is the suburbs.

PAULA. Regardless, even if this book is tucked away in a special section, how can you prevent that couple from talking honestly about their relationship?

CHASTITY. No good mother would ever expose her children to sexually explicit material.

PAULA. We're talking about families.

CHASTITY. Why should the rest of us adjust our values just to accommodate theirs?

PAULA. Because love is a rare bird.

(The words take **PAULA** *as much by surprise as they do* **CHASTITY.** *)*

CHASTITY. I beg your pardon?

PAULA. It's, um…hard enough trying to keep a marriage together, even if you feel obligated because of your children and your place in the community and the life you've built one brick at a time. You live on top of the world, but the walls still close in and you want to burst through the roof. But the elevator goes all the way to the basement. So you go through the motions while your soul bangs on the doors of your life screaming to get out. And half of the marriages you know explode like landmines, and your kids – your kids…So if anyone is capable of toughing it out and raising their children without screwing them up too much – even if it's two gay penguins – shouldn't we be celebrating that achievement? Shouldn't we support them any way we can?

(This give **CHASTITY** *pause.)*

CHASTITY. You screwed your husband's golf buddy, didn't you?

PAULA. Okay, we're done. *(***PAULA** *addresses the camera.)* Similar challenges to *And Tango Makes Three* have occurred in Shiloh, Illinois; Charlotte, North Carolina; Ankeny, Iowa; Saint Joseph, Missouri; Southwick, Massachusetts, and Calvert County, Maryland; not to mention all of the Middle East.

When we come back, the Ex-Gay Movement: does it work or is it just a place for homely gay men to get laid?

PART FIVE: LANDING

SCENE TWELVE

(The facade of 927 Fifth appears. The **MAN IN COVERALLS** *returns to install an iron cradle.)*

*(***PALE MALE** *swoops in, trying to assemble twigs on it.* **LOLA** *joins him.)*

PALE MALE. So.

LOLA. So.

PALE MALE. How do you like the new nest?

LOLA. Looks expensive.

PALE MALE. They put the pigeon spikes back in. And they added that cradle to catch all the debris.

LOLA. Hmm.

(more silence)

What have you been up to?

PALE MALE. The usual. Flying. Hunting.

LOLA. Kill anything good?

PALE MALE. The rats on Wall Street are too greasy, but the ones in Chinatown are delicious.

LOLA. Yeah, but an hour later you're hungry.

PALE MALE. How about you?

LOLA. I spent a month in New Jersey one day. Oh, and I finally saw the Statue of Liberty.

PALE MALE. That so?

LOLA. It's funny how you can live here so long and not do any of the touristy things.

PALE MALE. You see the kids?

LOLA. Gretel's at that tall building owned by the featherless bird with the nest on his head.

PALE MALE. Donald Trump.

LOLA. That's the one.

PALE MALE. Fancy.

LOLA. She always was a go-getter.

PALE MALE. The feather doesn't fall far from the nest.

LOLA. I'll take that as a compliment.

PALE MALE. It was meant as one. And Handsome?

LOLA. He's been called to the religious life. He spends all his time at that cathedral.

PALE MALE. Hmm. You don't think he's a gay, do you?

LOLA. The featherless bird who runs the place does look like a penguin. Would you mind if he were?

PALE MALE. It's none of my business. He's on his own now and I don't –

PALE MALE/LOLA. Fly backwards.

LOLA. I know.

(tension)

PALE MALE. Me, mostly, I've been hanging around the park.

LOLA. And how's that been?

*(**PALE MALE** concentrates.)*

PALE MALE. It makes me feel…

(He hesitates.)

LOLA. Yes…?

PALE MALE. Bad.

LOLA. Really?

PALE MALE. It's lonely at the top of the food chain.

LOLA. It is. *(She's encouraged, but wary.)* You've got your fans to keep you company.

PALE MALE. But they're not my friends.

LOLA. They saved our perch.

PALE MALE. Still, having so much time on my claws has given me a chance to brood.

LOLA. On what?

PALE MALE. How stubborn you are. How you never let me alone, just peck, peck, pecking to make me be the best me I can be. Even when you're not here I see you. You're my best friend, but sometimes you feel like my worst enemy.

LOLA. I feel like your worst enemy *because* I'm your best friend.

PALE MALE. Birds of a feather…

(She sits next to him.)

Look at them down there, gawking at us. Just waiting to see if we take to the air and mate. *(calling down to them)* Go away. Show's over. Shoo. Shoo.

LOLA. No, it's okay.

PALE MALE. You sure?

(She gives a tentative wave to the audience.)

(singing)

WHATEVER LOLA WANTS, LOLA GETS…

LOLA. That's a new song. What is it?

PALE MALE. Show tune.

LOLA. You're amazing.

PALE MALE. No, you're amazing.

LOLA. No, you.

PALE MALE. You.

LOLA. You.

PALE MALE. Okay, you.

*(They nestle as the lights dim, coming up on the **BIRDER** with his binoculars.)*

SCENE THIRTEEN

BIRDER. Forty grand – that's what it cost to put up those spikes and the cradle. If you add in the costs of the lawyers and the architects, it's closer to a hundred grand. I wished it had cost a million, for all the trouble those chuckleheads caused. If they had even bothered coming down here and looking through our viewfinders, they'd know that we can't even see into their windows. Not that we ever wanted to, anyway. But at least we got our hawks back. It's funny, though, that they call that iron net a cradle, 'cuz even though Pale Male and Lola have sex like five times a day…

(From offstage comes five-ten seconds of hawks screeching.)

…they haven't laid any eggs since. No one's quite sure why. It might be that Pale's getting old, but the fact that they stopped hatching the moment they changed the nest is an awfully big coincidence.

Some of the regulars think it's the way the pigeon spikes anchor the nest, others think it's a conspiracy – that the co-op put something toxic in that cradle. But Pale and Lola don't seem to mind. Unlike most hawk pairs, they don't separate in the off-season. They just hang out in the park together, which is not what he did with his other mates. I try not to anthropomorphize them, but they seem really happy together.

I can't say the same for Mister and Missus Paula Zahn. Cohen threw her out, just like he did to the hawks, then her romance with his golfing buddy went south when the buddy reconciled with his wife. But now, according to the *Daily News*, Zahn and her husband have put their divorce on hold. She hasn't moved back in, but they've been seen together at their kids' school functions.

Cohen even made a point of saying publicly what a devoted mother she is.

BIRDER. *(cont.)* Still, who wants to sign up for a lifetime of "you shoulda" and "why didn't you?" and "why do you leave wet towels on the bed?" What's the point of making a commitment to an institution that only has a fifty percent chance of survival?

But the other day, I was standing by the model boat pond, and I caught a glimpse of myself in the water, this not entirely repulsive guy surrounded by surveillance equipment. And I suddenly realized that I'd become someone who spends his free time watching someone else's life. Don't get me wrong – I'd rather watch reality than reality TV. But, still, I'm the guy who looked at chicks on a ledge while ignoring the chick standing next to him with the nice binoculars.

I'd say that's for the birds, but birds don't waste any time lookin' at us.

(He exits as the lights come up on the rocky landscape.)

SCENE FOURTEEN

(**ROY** *enters. He gives a nervous look around the rocky landscape past the water that gently laps the edge. Then, using his feet, he nudge-nudge-nudges a bowling ball-sized rock.*)

(*The* **ZOOKEEPER** *enters, watching as* **ROY** *sits on the rock he's been pushing.*)

(**SILO** *enters, looking anywhere but at* **ROY**.)

(*Seeing* **SILO**, **ROY** *clears his throat.* **SILO** *doesn't pay attention.* **ROY** *clears his throat again.*)

SILO. You sick?

ROY. No.

SILO. You don't swim enough. You've got to regulate your body temperature.

(**ROY** *coughs.*)

See? You spend too much time on land entertaining the featherless birds.

ROY. Silo!

SILO. What?

(**ROY** *jerks his head toward the rock.*)

Oh, no.

ROY. Yes.

SILO. Not again.

ROY. But it's that time of year. (*singing*)
BIRDS DO IT, BEES DO IT...

SILO. Roy!

(**ROY** *stops.*)

ROY. You used to love my songs.

SILO. No, I loved you. The songs I put up with.

(*tension*)

ROY. What did you say?

SILO. I'm sorry. I like that gravity song.

ROY. No. You said "loved".

SILO. Yes.

ROY. Past tense.

> (*more tension*)

SILO. I've met someone else.

> (**ROY** *can't speak.*)

> I'm sorry.

ROY. How…how can this happen?

SILO. I don't know. Who can say why?

ROY. No, I mean how can this happen? We live in a zoo. It's hardly an environment for making new friends.

SILO. I guess you were too busy being famous to notice.

ROY. It takes two to tango.

SILO. Please. Let's not fight.

ROY. Why? Would that be too audacious for you?

SILO. Don't start.

ROY. So does this nestwrecker have a name?

SILO. Scrappy.

ROY. Never heard of him. He must be new.

SILO. She is.

> (**ROY**'s *stunned.*)

> Roy…

ROY. You really hate that you're gay, don't you?

SILO. Don't psychoanalyze me. I happen to love her.

ROY. Why?

SILO. What kind of question is that?

ROY. Is it so hard to answer?

SILO. I never thought about it.

ROY. You think about everything.

> (*beat*)

SILO. She's fun. She's uncomplicated. She's…from San Diego.

ROY. I'm fun. I'm uncomplicated.

SILO. But loving you isn't.

ROY. What's that supposed to mean?

SILO. I never asked to be on the cover of a book. And no one asked me.

ROY. Do you realize what this is going to mean to the homophobes and the bigots? They're going to look at you and say, "See, that just proves that if you find the right female you can pray the gay away." Hallelujah!

SILO. Don't be ridiculous. That's like saying all females will cheat on their mates just because the one they call Paula Zahn did.

ROY. Apparently, she's not the only one.

SILO. Did it ever occur to you that the reason I was never comfortable calling myself gay was because I wasn't? That I stayed with you in spite of your gender?

ROY. Please. Straight guys don't repress their heterosexuality by trying to be gay.

SILO. Why not?

ROY. 'Cuz who the hell wants to be gay?

(Neither of them can believe he said it.)

SILO. I thought you did.

ROY. Please go.

SILO. I wasn't looking for love. And I certainly wasn't looking for a female.

ROY. I see. So it's okay because you didn't mean to break my heart.

(SILO steps away, then turns around.)

SILO. Listen, some of us are gay. Some of us are straight. And some of us...Isn't the world-wide-world wide enough for everybody?

ROY. This isn't the world-wide-world. It's a prison.

(SILO reaches for ROY, but ROY turns away, heading upstage to face a corner.)

(**SILO** *leaves. The lights change to indicate the passing of time as the* **ZOOKEEPER** *struggles to speak.*)

ZOOKEEPER. It was one of those perfectly-cloudless-this-hardly-happens-in-New-York kind of days. Tommy and I were on the deck of the Staten Island ferry coming into Manhattan, so we had a perfect view as the first plane swooped in like a giant bird before it crashed into the tower.

By the time Tommy got me home, I was so distraught he had to put me to bed and, well...I don't know what came over me, but I suddenly felt like I would die unless he was inside me. He didn't want to – I don't blame him. I had to get therapy for panic attacks before I could cross the river again.

What's so...stupid is that, as bad as all that was, Silo leaving Roy has been worse. It's ridiculous, I know. They're penguins. But I really wanted them to make it.

(*She breaks down. The* **BIRDER** *appears.*)

(*surprised*) Oh, dear God.

BIRDER. Sorry.

ZOOKEEPER. You scared me. (*She composes herself.*) May I help you?

BIRDER. I hope so. I, uh, know this is gonna sound a little weird...

ZOOKEEPER. Don't worry about that. Trust me.

BIRDER. Okay. Well, uh, do you happen to know which of the penguins are the gay ones?

(*The* **ZOOKEEPER** *erupts in tears.*)

Oh my God, are you okay?

ZOOKEEPER. I'm fine. Don't mind me.

BIRDER. It's all right.

ZOOKEEPER. I'm so embarrassed.

BIRDER. Don't worry. Would you like a tissue?

ZOOKEEPER. Do you have one?

BIRDER. No. But I got Altoids.

ZOOKEEPER. No thanks.

BIRDER. You sure? They're curiously strong.

ZOOKEEPER. I'm all right now. Well, I'm not all right *now*, but normally I'm all right. I mean, I'm usually a very stable person. Truly. I have a credit rating of seven-fifty.

BIRDER. That so? Mine's seven-twenty.

ZOOKEEPER. That's good, too. I try not to live beyond my means. My gay husb – my friend Tommy says that makes me un-American.

BIRDER. Yeah, you commmie pinko.

ZOOKEEPER. Anyway, I'm babbling like a crazy person with a shopping cart full of cans and a tin foil hat because I'm worried. About one of the gay penguins. That's him, over there. Roy. Ever since Silo left him, he's just stared at that wall. For months. Every night when I've left work, I've prayed that he wouldn't die of grief in the night. Because whoever says animals don't have feelings –

BIRDER/ZOOKEEPER. – hasn't spent much time around them.

(It's like he handed her a flower.)

BIRDER. You're gonna be all right.

ZOOKEEPER. Ya' think?

BIRDER. Absolutely. Of course, I'm just some random schmo, so I have zero credibility but – and this is gonna sound like a pick-up line, which it isn't, not that you're not totally pickupable, but you're way too vulnerable right now and you're dressed like a longshoreman and, frankly, you kinda smell a little like fish and am I still talking?

(She likes him.)

ZOOKEEPER. It's okay.

BIRDER. Anyway, the line that sounds like a pick-up line but isn't is that I've seen you.

ZOOKEEPER. Really? Here?

BIRDER. No. Over at the model boat pond. You were watching Pale Male.

ZOOKEEPER. And Lola.

BIRDER. You loaned me your binoculars.

ZOOKEEPER. I did?

BIRDER. Yeah.

ZOOKEEPER. Thank you.

BIRDER. Thank you. Belatedly. So my point is that only a really nice person would loan her binoculars to a stranger. And I can't believe that good things won't happen to such a nice person.

(*beat*)

ZOOKEEPER. I'm Jane.

BIRDER. Hi, I'm not gay. I mean, I'm Joe. My name is Joe.

ZOOKEEPER. Nice to meet you, not-gay Joe.

(*A figure appears in the corner.*)

BIRDER. So who's that one? The ex?

ZOOKEEPER. It looks like him.

BIRDER. How can you tell?

ZOOKEEPER. After awhile, you learn how to see.

BIRDER. So is it him?

ZOOKEEPER. No. It's her.

(**GROWN-UP TANGO** *emerges, no longer rambunctious, but still in her Yankees hat.*)

GROWN-UP TANGO. Papa?

ROY. Tango.

GROWN-UP TANGO. How are you?

ROY. (*hunting for the words*) Oh…

GROWN-UP TANGO. Sorry I haven't been around much.

ROY. You're busy. Swimming. Eating herring.

GROWN-UP TANGO. And you've been staring at a wall for months.

ROY. Everyone needs a hobby.

GROWN-UP TANGO. I've got something I want to tell you.

ROY. Are you okay? Is anything wrong?

GROWN-UP TANGO. Yes. No. I don't know.

ROY. What's happened?

(beat)

GROWN-UP TANGO. I think I'm in love.

ROY. Oh, but that's wonderful.

GROWN-UP TANGO. I don't know. I feel so confused. And yet not.

ROY. Sounds like love to me.

GROWN-UP TANGO. Does it? How do I know?

ROY. Does your heart sing so much that you can't contain the song, even though it may sound to everyone else like you're gargling a kazoo?

GROWN-UP TANGO. *(nodding)* We've started building a nest together.

ROY. Oh, so it's serious. Does this co-nester have a name?

GROWN-UP TANGO. Tazuni.

ROY. Tazuni. Never heard of him. He must be new.

GROWN-UP TANGO. She is.

*(**ROY** takes a moment to process his conflicting emotions.)*

ZOOKEEPER. *(to audience)* This is their true story, and of the hawks who nested on Paula Zahn's building, and of the birdbrained human behavior they each caused. All the facts are completely true.

BIRDER. Except birds can't talk.

*(**ROY** recovers.)*

ROY. Well. You'll have to have me over.

GROWN-UP TANGO. You'll have to leave your corner.

ROY. I see. So it's a ploy.

*(**GROWN-UP TANGO** takes her father's vestigial wing.)*

GROWN-UP TANGO. No. It's love.

(a heartbeat)

ROY. It is.

> (*As* **JANE** *and* **JOE** *look on, an image of two hawks appear upstage, their tails so red against the Everywhere of Blue.*)

END OF PLAY

www.ingramcontent.com/pod-product-compliance
Lightning Source LLC
Chambersburg PA
CBHW070643120726
47909CB00004B/1555